The Widower's Christmas Wish

Mail Order Brides of Dayton Falls

(Book One)

Copyright

Copyright 2018 Cheryl Wright

Dedication

To Margaret Tanner, my very dear friend and fellow author, for her enduring encouragement and friendship.

To Alan, my husband of over forty-eight years, who has been a relentless supporter of my writing and dreams for many years.

To You, my wonderful readers, who encourage me to continue writing these stories. It is such a joy knowing so many of you enjoy reading my stories as much as I love writing them for you.

Table of Contents

Chapter One

Westlake, Wyoming – 1880

Charlotte Montgomery gagged from the revolting odor coming from Joseph Rainer.

Mr Rainer, as he preferred to be called, was far from her choice of ideal husband.

Her father insisted she marry this horrible old man.

The deal had been made when she was just fifteen years old – the threat had been hanging over her head for five years already.

"Charlotte, get here now!"

They weren't even married yet, and he was already ordering her around. *What would it be like when they did marry?*

Her heart sank.

He sat in the parlor alone, much to Charlotte's dismay. Where had her parents gone? They were supposed to be her chaperone.

She'd endured more than enough of his groping and prepared herself for even more.

As she approached, he stood. "Ah, there you are my lovely." He sneered and pulled her close. His hands quickly went around her back. His pungent odor made her feel faint.

"Do you ever have a bath? Or change your clothing?" She was being bold, she knew she was, but she couldn't marry this vulgar man. Surely her parents would understand.

"Give me a kiss, my lovely." He leered at her and grabbed her face, pulling her toward him. Charlotte couldn't take it any longer, the smell was just too overpowering.

Without warning, but much to her delight, her breakfast made its way to the surface. All over Mr Rainer. He shoved her to the floor, away from him.

"Henry! Henry!" he screeched. "Look at what this horrible girl of yours has done to me!"

Her father came running. "Martha," he shouted, commanding his wife to attend. "Look what this stupid girl has done," he shouted. "Get her out of here! Now!"

Rainer was pacing the room. He pulled off his expensive, but now foul-smelling Morning Coat, and threw it across the room, then sat back down, furious at what had occurred.

Her mother flustered about. "Oh my." She pulled her daughter to her feet, pulling her close. "Let's get you cleaned up and into bed." Charlotte nodded meekly. She had no intention of disagreeing. At least it got her away from the despicable old man she was to wed.

Mother reached across and rang the bell for the servants.

"Ah, there you are Allie." She smiled at the petite young woman standing in front of her. "Miss Charlotte is unwell. She's, ah, lost her breakfast. Clean it up." She motioned to the mess, then swiftly left the room with her only child.

"That man is vulgar, Mother. The smell…" She gagged again at the thought. "I'm certain that's what made me ill."

Her mother frowned. "Get used to it. You *will* marry Mr Rainer. And soon. Your marriage is worth a lot of money to your father's business."

She near shoved her daughter up the stairs and toward the bathroom. "Clean yourself up and get to bed. We could lose everything if he finds out what made you ill."

Charlotte glared at her mother. *She couldn't believe the words coming from her mother's mouth.*

"And for goodness sakes, don't say a word to your father!"

Martha stormed out, leaving Charlotte wondering how on earth she would get out of this predicament.

* * *

"As much as I love you, dear brother," Abigail said. "I cannot continue to help you."

Sheriff Angus Doyle frowned. Their arrangement had worked so far. Since Sarah died giving birth to their daughter, Abigail had taken care of baby Emma.

The child was almost three now, but he needed a mother for Emma now that Abigail had other obligations.

She'd been supplying the Mercantile with her glorious baked goods for as long as he could remember. Now she was no longer content with that.

When old Mrs Hanson had retired, Abigail had gone and brought the darned bakery. Leaving him totally in the lurch.

He loved his sister, he really did. But he had an obligation to his tiny daughter. He was not capable of rearing a child himself, which is why he'd handed her over to Abigail when he'd lost his dear Sarah.

"What am I supposed to do? I can't quit. I don't know anything else." He took off his hat and scratched his head.

"I'm sorry, Angus, I really am. But this is the chance of a lifetime. Will and I are selling up and will be moving to Dead Creek." She fiddled with her skirts, not looking in his direction. "Very soon."

Angus swallowed hard. What was he going to do? Emma needed a mother more than she needed a father. "I thought you might just go in there every day?"

He knew in his heart they wouldn't – it was too far away.

"We might still be in Montana," she said. "But it's way too far to travel there daily."

A thought struck him. "You could take her with you. I would come and visit occasionally."

"Sounds like a good idea," she said. "But I can't run a full-time business with a small child running about."

Abigail stared down at her hands that were resting in her lap, not wanting to meet his gaze. "Have you thought of getting a mail order bride?"

His head shot up. "A mail order bride? Are you crazy, woman?"

"Not so crazy. Pete at the post office got a mail order bride early last year. They're very happy together. They even have a baby and another one on the way."

He stood suddenly. "Well it's the craziest thing I ever heard of. And it ain't gonna happen."

Abigail stood at the door, ready to leave. "Go talk to Pete. He says it's the best thing that ever happened to him."

Angus stared at his sister for long moments, then stomped from the room, leaving his sister to stare after him.

* * *

Charlotte sat with her back straight and her nose in the air.

It wasn't every day a young lady of her high standard visited a person such as Miss Bethany Wilde of the *Westlake Mail Order Bride Agency*

She was truly at the end of her tether. Mother and Father insisted she marry that revolting man. She couldn't do it. She couldn't go through life with him.

He truly was horrible. On top of all his other vices, he even ate with his mouth open!

The man was easily thirty-five years her senior.

She shuddered. There was no way in hades she could marry him, even if he was rich, and she would *live a life of luxury*, as her mother had put it.

But this wasn't about her, as her mother had also indicated. It was about her father's business thriving as a result of her forced marriage.

She wondered what they'd been promised to hand over the prize of their only daughter.

She could feel the bile rise in her throat and swallowed down on it. Just the thought of it made her ill.

It certainly wouldn't do to vomit over Miss Bethany. After all, the poor woman was trying to help her.

"I have five gentlemen looking for a mail order bride at this time," Miss Bethany told her as she handed over their handwritten letters. "Take a look and tell me what you think."

Charlotte leaned forward and took the crumpled papers from her. "Have you read these," she asked, not sure how she would choose.

"Of course, but I am not here to influence your decision. You need to choose for yourself." Miss Bethany sat back in her chair, and Charlotte could see the questions in her expression. Why would an heiress such as herself be looking to marry a man she'd never met?

It was blatantly clear to Charlotte, of course. She didn't want a man older than her father to bed her.

The older woman leaned forward. "Why?"

"Why?" Charlotte repeated, knowing full well what the other woman meant.

"Yes, why do you want to be a mail order bride? You come from a particularly good family and are in line for your father's fortune. Surely…"

Charlotte interrupted her. "My parents wish for me to marry Mr Joseph Rainer, who owns the bank." She sighed. "Yes, he is rich, but I am only twenty and he is at least fifty-five!" She sniffed, and wiped a stray tear from her eyes, despite her best intentions to stay strong. "How could they?"

"Oh, my dear girl! That is appalling." She ran to Charlotte's side and began to comfort her. "There have been whispers about Mr Rainer. He's been married twice before, did you know?" Charlotte shook her head, and the older woman continued. "His first wife just… disappeared. Wife number two is in the mental asylum." She straightened her back. "There is nothing wrong with Gwendolyn Rainer. I know her very well. He just wanted to get his hands on her money."

She winced, as though she too, were fighting back tears. "Yes, he is a vile creature, and we can't let him get his clutches on you, my dear!"

Charlotte gasped. She had no idea. Neither one of her parents had told her any of this. She felt faint with the shock.

She must have paled, since dear Miss Bethany rushed toward her with water.

She fanned Charlotte with some papers she'd scooped up off her desk. "Don't you worry, my dear. We will find you a decent young man to marry. Someone more your own age." She pushed two letters closer to Charlotte's hand. "These two may be more to your liking. Both wonderful young gentlemen going by their letters."

As Charlotte carefully read each letter, she wondered if she was doing the right thing. She loved her parents, but she simply couldn't marry Mr Rainer. She felt quite repulsed by the man.

How could she live the rest of her life with a man that she reviled? She simply couldn't, which meant she had no choice but to marry a complete stranger.

She read each letter carefully – for the third time. They both sounded like wonderful men. Like someone who would cherish her and look out for her. And let her be herself.

It only made the decision harder. Charlotte chewed at her bottom lip.

"Oh my dear girl! I know the decision is a hard one, and it's one that will affect your whole life, but don't harm yourself." Miss Bethany rubbed her hands across Charlotte's back, then hugged her tight.

Miss Bethany comforted her more than her own mother had ever done. It made tears come to her eyes.

Suddenly Charlotte straightened her back and set her resolve.

"This one," she said, pointing to the first letter. "He's a rancher. Out in the wide-open spaces. He could be good."

"Or it may be a lot of work for you, my dear," Miss Bethany added. "But he does sound nice."

"This second one – he's the sheriff," Charlotte said dreamily. "I'll bet he is handsome as well as strong. He would look after me, I just know it."

She pounced her finger on the sheriff's letter, over and over again. "I think I want the sheriff."

"You think, or you know?"

Of course, she had to be sure, because once she married this man, it was too late to take it back.

* * *

Charlotte lounged in bed longer than normal.

She simply couldn't face the day knowing she was to marry that horrid man. When, she had no idea,

but hopefully it would be long enough for her to get away.

"Good morning, Miss Charlotte," Allie said, sliding back the curtains.

Charlotte winced. "I'm really sorry," Allie whispered. "Your mother told me I had to get you up. Mr Rainer is coming for luncheon."

She winced again. "What time is it now, Allie?" Her mind was ticking over. How could she get out of this meeting? The truth was, she knew she couldn't. A terrible sadness overtook her. Without being told, it appeared her wedding day was getting ever closer.

"Eleven o'clock, Miss."

Allie laid out her clothes, and filled the basin with warm water, and then she was gone.

* * *

Such an influence did Mr Rainer have over her father, that he sat at the head of the table, a place normally reserved for Henry Montgomery.

He lifted his wine glass and offered a toast. "To my beautiful young bride. May we have a long and happy marriage." His voice was loaded with insincerity and Charlotte's heart rate accelerated. She felt faint, yet her parents noticed nothing amiss.

"To Joseph and Charlotte." Her father lifted his glass and clinked it with the other man's glass.

Rainer looked her up and down much like he was appraising an animal he was about to buy.

"The food is delicious my dear," he said to her mother, as though Martha had prepared it herself.

Her mother hadn't cooked a thing in her entire life. Why would she do that when she had servants to do every little thing for her?

Of course, when, *if* Charlotte married this despot, she too would have servants.

Her head began to ache.

"Please excuse me," she said. "I have an awful headache. I must lay down." She pushed her chair back and began to walk away.

"Charlotte, stop!" Rainer bellowed. She turned back and glared at the man. "You haven't heard the wonderful news yet. I came here to make an announcement." His face softened. "You and I – we're getting married on Saturday." He gave a smug smile.

"I, I…" Charlotte slid to the floor. The shock was too much to handle.

"Quick, get the smelling salts," she heard her mother say.

"I can't," she whispered to her mother.

Her mother waved the smelling salts under her nose again. "You can, and you *will*," she said between clenched teeth.

Martha helped her daughter onto a chair. Charlotte noticed Rainer didn't move from his seat to help her and continued to drink his expensive wine. She worried over the life she had ahead of her.

* * *

Four days.

Her wedding was to be in four days.

The seamstress had already been to fit Charlotte for her wedding dress, much to her disgust. And distress.

She'd cried the entire time the woman had measured her for her extravagantly expensive wedding gown.

"It's just nerves," Martha had told the anxious woman, who had nodded and accepted the explanation.

What else could she do? Charlotte's wedding gown was worth a lot of money to her.

She felt extremely guilty, but despite all the fuss and measuring, Charlotte would never wear that gown.

After the fitting, she stepped outside their mansion and headed into town. She fingered the expensive brooch sitting on her lapel, wondering how much it would bring.

She pulled her bonnet up over her head.

"Charlotte? Where are you going?"

She'd hoped to sneak out without anyone noticing. She should have known her mother would notice. "I'm going for a walk, Mother. I need some fresh air."

Martha nodded. "Be back in plenty of time for dinner. Mr Rainer is coming."

Again? Charlotte sighed. She needed to move fast.

She strolled down the main street, then looked about to ensure no one was watching. When it was clear, she turned into the alleyway her mother had told her never to enter.

Apparently, there was a criminal element that would steal the coat off your back. But today she was desperate enough to risk it.

Against her better judgement, she walked tentatively toward the horrid little pawn shop down the end of the alleyway. She stood outside pondering whether to enter. Her heart beat quickened knowing she really had no choice.

If she was to get away, she had to sell her expensive brooch.

She stared at the man standing in front of her. He snatched the brooch of her hands, and she worried she'd never see it again.

He looked her up and down, then fingered the brooch. Then he picked up his magnifying glass to get a better look.

He whistled. "Where did you get this, little lady?" he asked. *Did he think she'd stolen it?*

She took offense at the question. "It's mine," she said in a huff. "A birthday gift from my parents."

He nodded. "If you say so." The sneer on his face told her he didn't believe a word of it.

He tapped his finger on the shiny piece of jewelry firmly entrenched in his hands. "I can't give you too much for this piece," he said, studying it again. "I won't be able to sell it."

She snatched it out of his hands. "Good day to you, Sir," she said, then turned to walk out of the store.

"Wait a minute, little lady." He scratched his head. "That's a good lookin' piece and I want it."

She turned back toward the frightening man standing before her. She looked him up and down, and for the first time noticed the pistol sitting at his waist.

Would he just take her brooch without paying? She swallowed hard.

"Make me an offer, Sir," she said, her heart racing and her hands clammy.

He pulled a bundle of notes from under the counter. "It's the best I can do."

Against her better judgement, she shook her head. "It's not enough for… what I need," she said, and turned to walk away.

She knew it was a bad idea coming here. So why did she do it? Because she was desperate, and she knew it.

"Wait!" he bellowed at her as she opened the door to leave.

As she stared at him, he leaned down and snatched up another handful of notes. "Will this be enough? I can't offer you anymore. Stolen jewelry is difficult to sell."

"It's not stolen," she spat. "I told you, it was a gift." She snatched the additional money from his hands and with reluctance passed over the sparkling diamond brooch. Her favorite. "It's enough for what I need." She pushed the notes into her pocketbook and fled from the disarming store.

She almost ran from the alleyway and leaned against a wall, trying to catch her breath. Tomorrow

Charlotte would buy her train ticket to Dayton Falls, Montana.

* * *

"It's highly unusual," Miss Bethany said. "But these are dire circumstances."

Charlotte nodded. "I have my railway ticket, and I'll leave in the morning. Otherwise, I'll be married to that vile man in two days."

She straightened her back. She wouldn't cry in front of this kind lady again.

"He won't know you're coming. You haven't even had time to answer his letter." Miss Bethany paced the floor. "This is highly unusual," she said again, her voice getting higher with every sentence she spoke.

"I'll just try and find him once I've arrived," Charlotte said. "The town can't be that big."

Miss Bethany stared at her open-mouthed. "You can't be serious? You must be collected, you can't go wandering around in a strange place." She put her hand to her head. "Just let me think a minute or two."

She stood still for a moment, then continued to pace the room.

"Oh, I have an idea," she said, grinning broadly. "Show me your ticket, Charlotte."

Charlotte handed over the ticket, and Miss Bethany wrote down the details.

"I shall send a telegram and let him know when you're arriving." She stared at Charlotte as if looking for acceptance of her idea.

Charlotte nodded, relieved everything was in order.

* * *

Charlotte packed as much of her clothing into her overnight bag as she could manage.

She needed to have at least two changes of day dresses, and of course, undergarments. But she had to travel light. When she snuck out of the house at the crack of dawn, she would have no one to carry her bags, and indeed, she didn't want any help.

She dare not utilize any of the servants, as that would implicate them when her parents discovered she was gone.

She looked around her huge bedroom. She'd spent most of her life in this room. As Miss Bethany had said, she was very privileged. Not many young women of her age enjoyed the luxuries she'd had endowed on her. Indeed, most women of any age did not receive the indulgences she saw as normal.

She opened drawers and cupboards, deciding what she needed to take. She was going to miss all this, and she knew her new life would be very different to her current life.

And yet, she knew she had to leave.

She must leave, and the time to leave was near. She had no choice.

* * *

Charlotte headed to the railway station at the crack of dawn.

The house was quiet, which meant she had to be extra careful not to make a sound. The trip to Montana was going to be long and tiring. She couldn't imagine how awful she would smell after several days on the train! She was pleased she'd packed her lavender water.

She slid through the night like a cat burglar, not wanting anyone to know she'd been there.

It was eerie at that early hour. More eerie than she'd anticipated. Charlotte had never been outside at this ungodly hour and hoped she never did again.

By the time she arrived at the train station, she was petrified. Every sound, every movement startled her. In nearly every case it was either birds or other creatures such as cats, going about their nocturnal business.

She was in near-panic by the time she found the correct platform but straightened her back as she'd been taught to do. It wouldn't do to have others see her slouching.

At the last moment she thought to adjust her bonnet, to cover her face. The last thing she needed was for someone to recognize her and tell her father where she was headed.

"All aboard!"

Charlotte gasped. She hadn't realized how late it was already and hurried to her carriage. The conductor checked her ticket and let her pass.

She walked up and down the aisle until she found her seat. Once seated she held her bag tightly on her lap. It contained all her worldly possessions and she didn't know what she'd do without them.

She stared out the window and saw people running. Her train was about to depart. Charlotte Montgomery was about to begin her new life.

* * *

Miss Bethany sent the following telegram three hours after Charlotte's train departed:

To Sheriff Angus Doyle, Dayton Falls, Montana.

Miss Charlotte Montgomery arriving Monday 4 o'clock stop

please collect from train station stop

situation dire stop

Signed Miss Bethany Wilde – Westlake Mail Order Bride Agency

Angus read the note over and over again. "But, but I don't know anything about her," he said to his sister. "I haven't had a chance to tell her about young Emma either."

He screwed up the telegram as he sunk down into a chair. "What am I going to do now?"

Abigail stared at him. "What you are going to do, dear brother, is collect her from the station on Monday afternoon."

"So much for not getting a mail order bride," she said under her breath.

He glared at her. "I heard that. Besides, you left me no choice. What else was I going to do?"

Abigail shrugged her shoulders. "I have no idea. But what's done is done. Looks like you're getting married on Monday."

"Get in the cell, you filthy…" The deputy stared at Abigail. "Sorry Miss Abigail. I didn't know you was there."

Abigail smiled, then hugged her brother. "I better let you get back to work. I can't wait to meet your bride," she said, then left the Sheriff's Office smiling.

Chapter Two

Sheriff Angus Doyle arrived at the station a little later than anticipated. There was always some riff-raff there to mess up his day.

He looked about trying to spot his soon-to-be-bride but had no luck. He had no idea what she looked like, and no way to identify her.

He stood on the platform and waited for the crowd to disperse.

Then waited.

And waited.

As the station cleared, he was becoming concerned. He unruffled the telegram he'd screwed up and checked the day and time. *Yep, this was the right train.*

He frowned.

After about fifteen minutes more Sheriff Doyle decided to investigate. He approached the conductor, and together they began to search the carriages.

The third carriage yielded results. They found a young woman sound asleep in her compartment, holding tightly to her carpetbag.

Angus stood over her, looking her up and down.

Her blonde hair was somewhat disheveled but pulled back into a plait. Her clothes were splattered with soot, but her face was pure white.

The scent of lavender water filled his nostrils.

She was beautiful, but pale and drawn. He wasn't sure if that was a result of the long trip, or whether she was ill.

He felt guilty for thinking it, but how could she look after Emma if she was ill? He shook his head, trying to rid himself of the thought.

"Miss, wake up," the conductor said.

She didn't budge.

"Miss," he said more loudly. "You need to wake up Miss."

He looked to the sheriff.

"Charlotte?" Sheriff Doyle said rather assertively. When that didn't work he touched her shoulder. "Charlotte, wake up," he yelled.

"Wha…?"

The young woman woke in a fright.

"Are you Charlotte Montgomery," Angus asked.

She rubbed at her eyes and looked up at the two men standing over her,

"I, I'm Charlotte Montgomery," she said warily, then looked him up and down. "Ooooh, you're the sheriff!"

She looked mighty pleased to see him, which warmed his heart.

He'd planned to whisk her off to the preacher, and for the pair to marry immediately. But that was put on hold. There was no way he could marry her like this. Her clothes needed to be cleaned up, and her hair was a mess.

He reached over and grabbed her bag. Her grip was strong, and she didn't want to let go. "I'll take your bag, Miss Montgomery."

Her lips parted slightly, and she nodded, but still held tight.

He zoned in on those lips and took a deep breath. It was so long since he'd been with a woman. He had to remember she was here to look after his daughter – that was her main reason for being here. At least in his mind.

Still, having a wife did have other benefits.

"I have a wagon out front. We should leave." He dipped his hat, thanked the conductor, and helped Charlotte to her feet.

"First things first," he told her. "You probably need a long hot bath."

She nodded again. If he hadn't heard her speak earlier, he'd think her mute.

"I'll take you to Mrs Foggerty's boarding house. You can have a bath there and sleep the night." He led her out to the wagon, and held her around her tiny waist, helping her up the steps. "Can't get married with you looking like this," he told her.

Angus wondered how long it was since she'd eaten.

Once she was settled, he climbed up and they started their journey.

They traveled through the center of town, and it wasn't long before they arrived at Mrs Foggerty's boarding house. "Wait here," Angus told her. "I'll check if there are any rooms available."

He was halfway off the wagon when Charlotte spoke. "I thought I'd be staying with you," she said quietly.

He was shocked to say the least. "Not until we're married, Miss Montgomery," he said abruptly.

Her face fell, and he thought she was going to turn on the water works, but to his surprise, she didn't.

He knocked on the door, and Mrs Foggerty opened the door slightly and looked out. "Ah Angus! Good afternoon to you."

She pulled the door open wider and stared at the young woman on the wagon. "This is Miss Charlotte Montgomery," Angus told the elderly woman. "She's to be my bride," he said. "She's had a long trying voyage."

"Then I shall get her cleaned up and presentable. When is the ceremony?"

The sheriff's face relaxed. "It was to be shortly, but I can't take my bride to the preacher looking like this."

He stared across at Charlotte and watched as a tear rolled down her cheek. "Not that it's her fault," he said loudly. "Those trains make such a mess of the passengers." He winked at Mrs Foggerty. He was certain she understood his intentions.

He didn't want his bride to be upset with him.

"Righto then. Bring her in, Angus."

He had known Mrs Foggerty for as long as he could remember. She'd been an old lady when he was a young tacker. At least to his mind.

He hated to think how old she was now and had no intentions of asking her.

She would sort out his new bride, and ensure she was presentable for the ceremony tomorrow.

He reached up and held her by the waist, then lifted her gently to the ground. She stood in front of him and stared into his eyes – hers were mesmerizing, and he was frozen to the spot.

If Mrs Foggerty hadn't been standing nearby, he didn't know what might have happened. He reached up and grabbed the carpetbag that had been clutched so tightly earlier.

"I'll be back in the morning," he said, reaching into his pocket and handing Mrs Foggerty some coins.

She nodded, took Charlotte in hand, then guided her into the house.

* * *

It all happened so quickly.

Charlotte's mind was in a whirl. One minute she was sitting in that ghastly train, then she was atop a wagon, and now she was in a stranger's house.

"Florence Foggerty, my dear," the older woman said. "This is your room for the night. Get yourself settled, and then I'll organise a nice hot bath for you."

She fiddled with her skirts, then turned to leave the room. "I'll collect you shortly, Miss Montgomery." She then turned to leave the room.

"Miss Foggerty," Charlotte said quietly. The older woman turned to back toward her. "I'm sorry I look so horrid. I've been on that wretched train for days."

The older woman nodded. "Don't you worry, my dear. Your groom understands, that's why he brought you here."

Charlotte opened the carpetbag to ensure her possessions were all still there. She lay her two dresses out on the bed, hoping to remove the creases. She'd never seen her clothing so disheveled.

She had to wear one of those dresses as her wedding gown. It was incomparable to the gown her mother was having made, but one of these would have to do. She had no other choice.

For a moment, Charlotte wondered if Mother and Father were worried about her. She didn't care what that awful Mr Rainer thought. She was just relieved that she'd escaped his horrid clutches.

Charlotte was startled by a tap on the door a short time later. "May I enter?"

She opened the door.

"Don't take this the wrong way, but you really are a mess my dear." She retreated from the room. "Follow me. We'll get you cleaned up and looking beautiful for your new husband." She smiled, the first time Charlotte had seen anything except a scowl.

"He's a wonderful man, our sheriff," she said. "You won't be sorry." She took Charlotte to a small room off the kitchen and closed the door behind them.

"It looks heavenly," Charlotte exclaimed. She was bone weary and couldn't think of anything more appealing right now.

The bath was full of bubbles, and she put her hand in the water to feel the temperature. "Oooh, it's very hot!"

Mrs Foggerty frowned. "And you, my dear, are very dirty."

She handed Charlotte a towel and a face towel and left the room.

Charlotte let her filthy clothes slide to the floor. She put first one foot, then the other into the hot soapy water, then slid down beneath the bubbles.

Heaven.

She let her hair down and slid below the water and washed it. She couldn't remember a time when she'd felt so wretched. And to be called dirty? She cringed.

Mother would have a fit.

She saturated the face cloth and cleaned her face. She looked down into the now putrid water. *Was she really that dirty?*

She felt the heat creep up her face. What must Angus Doyle think of her? No wonder he wasn't prepared to marry her like that. Her eyes filled with tears at the thought.

She was a young woman from a well-to-do Wyoming family. At least he wasn't aware of that fact. He would be disgusted.

Charlotte sobbed. Perhaps he already was.

She gasped.

Would he even come back for her?

If he didn't, what would she do then? She had no skills to speak of. She could only bake because cook would sneak her into the kitchen when Mother wasn't around.

"Supper's almost ready, Charlotte. Miss Montgomery. Are you almost finished?"

She wanted to stay there forever. She felt relaxed in that wonderful bath, but she had to get out sometime. "Coming Mrs Foggerty. I won't be long, I promise."

* * *

Charlotte brushed her hair and tied it back.

Today was the day she was getting married. She could barely believe she was a mail order bride. She'd heard of such things, but never dreamed she'd be so desperate as to become one herself.

But when one needed to get out of a dire situation, it was a good alternative.

She stood in the middle of the room in her chemise and drawers, with both dresses laid out on the bed.

"Charlotte, my dear," Mrs Foggerty called. "Are you almost ready? The sheriff will be here any minute now!"

Charlotte gasped. "I, I can't decide which dress to wear."

She opened the door a crack and looked around at the other woman. "Can you help me choose, please?"

Just then, there was a knock at the front door.

"Oh my gosh, it's the sheriff," Mrs Foggerty exclaimed. "You can't come in, she's not ready!" She peered around the door and Charlotte jumped back so her groom couldn't see her in her state of undress.

"That is so kind of her," she heard the older woman say. "I'm sure she'll be thrilled."

She heard mumblings from Angus but couldn't make out what he was saying. Then the door was tightly closed.

"You'll never believe this, my dear," Mrs Foggerty said as she opened the bedroom door slightly. "May I come in? I come bearing gifts."

Charlotte could hear the joy in her voice. "I prayed for a miracle for you, and Our Dear Lord answered."

Mrs Foggerty pushed a large box toward her. "Open it, my dear." She was grinning broadly.

Charlotte gently lifted the lid and peaked inside. "Oh my! It's a wedding dress!" She was speechless and stood there staring.

"It belongs to the sheriff's sister. She wanted you to have a proper wedding dress." She patted Charlotte's hand. "That was very kind of her."

They pulled the dress out of the box, and Charlotte held it up against herself. "I think it might fit," she said quietly.

She sat on the edge of the bed and pulled the dress up around herself.

"Turn around and I'll close the fastenings for you. Oh my gosh, look at this beautiful embroidery."

Charlotte stared at her image in the mirror, as Mrs Foggerty lifted the short veil onto her head and secured it.

She leaned in close to the younger woman and whispered in her ear. "You look beautiful, my dear. A far cry from the way you arrived yesterday."

Charlotte could have sworn Mrs Foggerty had tears in her eyes, but she was surely mistaken.

"Quickly now, pack up your bag and I'll escort you out to your groom."

As Charlotte snatched up her few meagre belongings, Mrs Foggerty had a few words of wisdom. "You look after our Angus. He's a wonderful man, and he'll take good care of you." She pulled Charlotte in for a hug. "Look after his manly needs, and everything will be alright."

She watched the heat creep into the older woman's cheeks. Charlotte frowned. She wasn't sure what that meant but didn't feel disposed to ask.

"Have his meals ready when he gets home and give him lots of babies. That's all a man can ask for."

Charlotte let out a long sigh. "I will do my best."

She was pushed out of the front door, where her beaming groom-to-be was waiting. Mrs Foggerty ran to him and pulled him into a big bear hug.

"Congratulations my dear boy. I know you will both be very happy."

Angus took both her hands and stood there looking her up and down. "You look amazing," he said quietly. "My beautiful bride." His voice broke, and Charlotte wondered how he could be so emotional about marrying a complete stranger.

Right now, at this moment, she felt nothing. Nothing at all – except for relief that in a few minutes she would be completely free of Joseph Rainer.

Once she was married to Sheriff Angus Doyle, there was nothing anyone could do to make her marry that filthy old man.

She looked up and Angus was staring into her eyes. His hands slid to her waist, and he lifted her up onto the wagon. He placed her dirty carpetbag on the back of the wagon.

He climbed aboard, then took up the reins. "Are you ready to become Mrs Doyle," he asked grinning. "Not long now."

She nodded, but Charlotte felt strangely impassive. She stared at the profile of the man she was to shortly marry.

He seemed like a good man, and Mrs Foggerty had said he was. Who was she to differ?

Soon they were on their way to the church, where the preacher would marry them.

Chapter Three

Charlotte was shaking. He knew she would be nervous, but he could see her trembling. What was she afraid of?

The ceremony was practically over, and they'd each said their vows and made promises to each other.

They were almost there.

"I now pronounce you man and wife."

Angus had been coming to this church all his life and knew the preacher well. When he'd explained the situation yesterday, he'd tried to talk Angus out of marrying a young woman he'd never met, but it didn't sway him.

Charlotte let out a loud sigh. Angus turned and gazed at her. *What was she thinking?* This petite young woman whom he didn't even know less than twenty hours ago.

She stared into his eyes, and he watched as they took in every detail of his face.

He wanted to reach out and touch her cheek, but that would never do. Not in church, anyway. She would likely swipe his hand away.

"You may kiss your bride now." The preacher's words were music to his ears. He wanted so badly to kiss the beauty standing next to him, but should he? Would she even let him?

Again, she stared into his eyes. This time she looked terrified, and her bottom lip trembled.

He held both her hands gently and leaned forward. As he moved toward her lips, she flinched, so he changed direction and lightly kissed her cheek instead.

They were now so close he heard her try to stifle a gasp. It didn't quite work.

He winked at her, as though trying to reassure her she was safe. That he wouldn't hurt her.

She nodded so gently he almost missed it. It was as though she was saying she understood.

They turned to leave the little chapel, and he noticed Mrs Foggerty sitting in the pews. There were a few other people there too, mostly relatives, but a few close friends.

This was a second marriage for him, but he was certain it was her first time.

For a moment he felt sad that she had no one here to see her married. Her parents particularly – he would have liked to meet them. He had no idea of her situation, but she must have been desperate to get away from them. Miss Bethany had said the situation was dire.

Otherwise, why would a beautiful, cultured woman like her become a mail order bride?

Why would any woman become a mail order bride?

Not that he had any experience in such things, but surely there must be an element of danger in their lives to totally uproot their lives and leave their family to marry a complete stranger?

Often in a state far from where they lived, such as his new wife had done.

They stood together outside the chapel, and a small crowd gathered around them throwing rice on them. Angus reached up and pulled pieces of rice from her hair. Touching her made him shiver.

His sister came up and kissed him on the cheek. "This is my sister Abigail," Angus told her. "It's her dress you're wearing," he whispered so no one else could hear.

"Thank you very much," she said to Abigail. "It's very beautiful."

Abigail suddenly pulled her into a big hug. "I'm so glad to finally have a sister," she said, as her tears ran onto Charlotte's shoulder. "Anything you need, you just ask."

She pulled back then stared into Charlotte's face. "Oh, you don't look very old."

"I'm twenty! I'm not a baby," Charlotte told her in no uncertain terms.

Angus grinned at the shenanigans of his sister. It was so Abigail.

"We've put together a small celebration," Mrs Foggerty said. "At Abigail's house. Nothing fancy, just something to celebrate your marriage."

He took Charlotte by the hand. "That's very sweet. Thank you both." He guided Charlotte to the wagon, and grabbed her around the waist, lifting her up onto the wagon.

He wasn't sure what it was, but every time he touched her, warmth filled him.

He stared at her face. She was incredibly beautiful. All that soot and dirt yesterday totally covered her beauty. He'd been certain there was a striking woman under all that mess, and he'd been right.

He pulled his gaze away and got back to the task at hand. "My sister lives out of town. Not far from my property." He looked across at her. "Er, our property." He grinned. He wasn't sure he'd ever get used to being married and thinking of them as a couple.

He hadn't had much time to get used to the idea of being married, and it was totally surreal.

He lifted the reins and headed the horses toward his sister's farm.

* * *

It was a small affair, but Charlotte was appreciative of the gesture.

Abigail's farm was lovely. It was a log cabin and looked superb from the outside. Inside it was cozy. There were four chairs scattered around the room, each with cushions made by Abigail.

The fire place was large, with logs sitting in the cavity, as well as a box of fresh fire wood next to it.

There was a lantern on the low table, which sat in the middle of the room.

She couldn't help but stare.

She gasped when Angus suddenly spoke. "Beautiful, isn't it?" He squeezed her hand, and she felt a thrill run up her arm.

"It truly is," she said quietly.

"Follow me," he said. "Abigail has a magnificent kitchen."

They stood in the doorway, and Charlotte stared at the wood stove. She'd never seen one so big. Not even at her parent's home.

"My sister bakes for the Mercantile. She supplies them twice a week, always with a big variety."

"How wonderful." But it wasn't really wonderful, Charlotte decided, because it meant Abigail was a fantastic cook, and Angus would soon realize she wasn't so good.

She'd only learned to bake a few things, mainly a variety of cakes such as election cake, chocolate cake, and her favorite, Almond Crumble Cake.

Cook could only teach her when there was time, so she hadn't learned a lot.

Angus put his arm around her and squeezed her shoulder. "It's pretty impressive, eh? I'm sorry to say your kitchen doesn't match this one."

"I've set everything up out the back," Abigail said, interrupting their discussion. "Bring her out back, big brother." She wandered off to greet some of the guests who had just arrived, then turned back.

"No, wait," Abigail said. "Have you told her yet?" She frowned at her brother.

"Haven't had a chance," he said, glaring at his sister.

Charlotte was confused. *What were they talking about?*

Angus sighed. "There's something I have to show you, Charlotte," he said. "I'm sorry, but with such short notice, I didn't get a chance to tell you." He took her by the hand and guided her through the cabin.

They stopped at a room where a small child was sleeping in a cot. "Your sister has a baby!" she whispered, glee in her voice.

He gazed down at her, his eyes penetrating hers. "Emma is mine," he said. "Her mother died birthing her." He stared at her, waiting for some sort of response, but none came. "Abigail has been looking after Emma since her birth, but she's moving away soon."

He turned his head, so she couldn't see his face. "She's the reason I needed a wife," he said quietly.

Charlotte felt betrayed. He brought her all the way here to look after his child? And he didn't tell her?

She was fuming.

"To be fair," he said, staring at her. "I was going to tell you in my next letter. But you were suddenly here without notice."

She nodded. He was right. This was her fault entirely.

Actually, it wasn't. She was forced to run and blamed her parents and Mr Rainer for her situation.

She took a deep breath. Our Dear Lord was challenging her. Why else would he put her in this situation? He had placed her with a dear man. A man in great need.

"I'm sure it will all work out," Charlotte told him, forcing herself to smile. "How old is Emma?"

He breathed a sigh of relief. It was so great, Charlotte heard it. "Nearly three."

"Let's go out and greet our guests," he said, taking his new wife by the hand. "Papa!" The little voice forced them to turn back.

Little arms went up for her dear Papa to lift her out of the cot. She hugged him tight when he held her close.

Charlotte studied his face. His muscles had loosened, and his expression was softer. She could see how much he loved his little girl.

She glanced across at Emma and saw her watching Charlotte's every move, staring into her face.

"Who's dat?" Emma asked.

Angus grinned. "This is your new Mama," he told the child. "Say hello."

Charlotte was shocked. Mama? Her?

Emma stared at her again but didn't say a word.

"Say hello to Mama, Emma." Angus was persistent, and finally was rewarded.

"Hello Mama." Emma buried her face in her father's shoulder, and Angus carried her outside.

Charlotte took in the view before her, trying not to stare at the child. It was magnificent, she knew it was, but she couldn't get her new situation out of her mind.

She had married not an hour ago, and suddenly she'd become a mother too. It was all so overwhelming.

"Wonderful, isn't it?" Angus said, ignoring the fact he had a small child in his arms. "My sister and her husband William certainly chose a great place to live." He looked at her sideways. "But now they're leaving." He scowled at his sister.

"Now that everyone is here," William said, "It is time to celebrate the marriage of Charlotte and Angus. May they have plenty of babes." Everyone laughed, and Charlotte felt the heat creep up her face.

As of this moment, she wasn't certain how babies got in a woman's belly, so it was unlikely she'd ever have any.

* * *

It was almost dark by the time they arrived at Angus's house.

As he'd told her, it wasn't very far from Abigail and William's place, and she would learn to drive a wagon, so she could visit her sister-in-law – while they were still living near by anyway.

At least that's what Angus said. She wasn't sure she'd ever manage to do that.

He pulled up near the front door and helped her down, along with the child. Sometimes she thought he just liked to hold her, rather than it being a necessity.

It did feel nice though, having her big strong handsome husband hold her like that and swing her down off the wagon. She felt safe.

He escorted her up onto the porch, then told her to wait there with Emma. "I'll go and light the lantern. I don't want you falling over on your wedding night."

From what she could see in the semi-darkness, the cabin looked nice. Not as big as his sister's, but nice all the same.

The rooms were somewhat smaller too, but Abigail and William seemed to live in a mansion, not as palatial as where she used to live, though. The baking brought in quite a nice sum, according to Angus.

"I'm tired Mama," a little voice said through the darkness as she reached up and tugged Charlotte's hand. It had been a long day for her, and she could only imagine what it would feel like to an almost three-year-old.

Abigail hadn't wasted any time handing the child over, and her cot was strapped to the back of the wagon. Charlotte thought at the least, Emma would be given time to get to know her.

But Abigail decided a clean break was needed, and here they were.

The house lit up from the lanterns, and Angus untied the cot and carried it into what had always been intended as Emma's room. At least that's what he told her.

Charlotte lifted the bag holding the child's clothing and other possessions from the wagon and headed into the house with Emma.

Poor little mite was almost asleep on Charlotte's shoulder. She undressed the child in her new room and replaced her clothes with her night wear.

She was asleep the moment her little head hit the pillow.

Charlotte wandered around the cabin, getting to know where she was going to live for the rest of her life.

The thought had her frozen in her tracks. For just a moment she mourned having left her family and their wealth. But then she came to her senses when a vision of Joseph Rainer trying to kiss her came into her mind.

She shuddered.

Angus returned to the cabin after settling the horses for the night. It was getting quite late, and it was time for bed.

Charlotte stood in the doorway to the bedroom. Their bedroom. The only room left to sleep in.

She took a few tentative steps into the room. The bed looked heavenly. After many days on a rickety train, she was ready for a decent sleep.

The bed at Mrs Foggerty's was passable, but not luxurious like she was used to. She sat on the edge of the double bed in front of her. It felt soft enough.

She pushed at it with her hands, then pulled back the cover slightly.

It did feel comfortable.

"Having second thoughts?" Angus stared at her. It was too late for second thoughts. She'd married him and there was no going back.

He stood in front of her. "We haven't had a chance to get to know each other," he said quietly as he pulled her close against him.

She felt warmth spread through her body.

His arms went up around her, and she rested her head on his shoulder. It felt nice, but he was a complete stranger. She shouldn't feel so comfortable with him.

"It's late," he said after a few minutes of standing like that together. "I'm sure you're exhausted."

She sighed. "I am. It was a long trip from Wyoming to here."

She stared at the bed, as though watching it would turn it into two beds.

Angus offered to leave the room while she prepared for sleep.

"I, I can't undo the fastenings myself," she said, as she felt heat creep up her face.

Now she was relying on a stranger to undress her. She felt like a harlot.

He stared into her eyes, then a slow smile came to his face. "Turn around." He held her shoulders, then gently turned her.

One by one he unbuttoned the tiny fastenings. She felt a thrill every time he touched her bare skin.

"All finished," he finally said, and pulled her gently against him. She felt his lips softly touch her bare shoulder. "I'll be back in ten minutes," he said quietly, then left the room.

The moment he was gone, she let the wedding gown fall to the ground, then scrambled for her carpetbag, pulling out her nightwear. It was no sooner over her head, than her new husband returned.

She scooped up the gown and lay it across a chair. She'd sort it out in the morning.

She quickly jumped into bed.

"I normally sleep naked," he told her quietly. "But since all this is new to you, I'll wear drawers tonight."

She was shocked, but knew he was mocking her because of the big grin on his face. She didn't answer but pulled the covers up over her face.

He slid into bed quietly and startled her when he reached out and pulled her close to him. "Is it alright if I hold my wife close tonight?" he asked.

She froze. She wasn't sure what was expected of her, since her mother hadn't explained. Perhaps she'd intended to tell Charlotte on her wedding day.

"I, I've never been in bed with a man before," Charlotte said honestly, ensuring he understood.

She felt him tighten his grip. "That needs to change," he said. "But not tonight. We'll take it slowly."

She sighed. At least tonight she had a reprieve, but for how long?

Chapter Four

Charlotte slowly opened her eyes and looked around.

She didn't know where she was and sat up suddenly. She heard a moan from beside her and it all came crashing back.

Her entire life had changed yesterday. Married *and* a mother within hours. And now here she was laying in bed with her new husband.

Her very handsome husband.

He'd held her close all night – she remembered now. Recalled the feelings she'd had being in his arms, feeling his hard body against hers, and the way she'd felt at home with him.

"Good morning, wife of mine." His voice was deep and sexy. Every time he spoke it did things to her. She wasn't sure if that was a good thing or not.

She slowly climbed out of bed. "Good morning," she said, a little less cheery than she probably should be.

A large hand snaked around her waist and pulled her back. "Time for a quick cuddle?" She turned to see him grinning at her.

"Papa! Mama!" A little voice yelled to be let out of the cot.

He let go suddenly. "The joys of having a child." He sighed. "I guess there will be no cuddling." Instead he kissed her lips lightly, taking Charlotte by surprise.

The kiss was unexpected, and Charlotte was left reeling by the tingle that lingered on her lips.

He stared into her eyes, no doubt daring her to protest. She had no intention of it. He was her lawful husband, and he had every right to kiss her, if her mother's words were anything to go by.

"You must be hungry," she said suddenly, jumping out of bed. "I'm sure Emma is too."

Charlotte pulled a robe around herself and headed to little Emma's room. She was rewarded with a huge grin as the little arms went up in the air. "Mama!"

"Hello sweetheart," Charlotte said gently. "Mama's here." She still couldn't get her head around it but forced herself to use her new title.

"So is Papa!" Angus strolled into the room and Emma forced herself into his big strong arms. Charlotte watched on as he held his daughter tight.

It must have been heart-breaking to have been separated from her for so long. All that was about to change – the child deserved to be with her father, and Angus deserved to have his daughter with him.

Suddenly Emma's face looked pained. "Papa, I have to go," she said urgently. Except the poor child had no idea where the privy was. For that matter, neither did Charlotte.

Angus pointed them in the right direction, and they both headed out.

When they returned, Charlotte felt so much better, and could only imagine how the little girl was feeling.

"Into your room, young lady, and we'll get you dressed."

Angus stood back and watched, grinning at her.

"What?" She'd done nothing to get that reaction. Or had she?

He pulled her close and whispered in her ear. "You're very cute when you're being Mama."

She gasped. Is that what she was doing?

She tried to pull out of his arms, but he held tight. "I have to get your daughter dressed. Let go."

But he didn't want to and continued to whisper. "I like holding you like this. Don't you like it?" He frowned.

She let herself go limp against him. "I do," she said. "But I have to get Emma dressed. Please."

He dropped his arms from around her and she suddenly felt bereft, as though a part of her had been removed.

* * *

Angus quickly dressed and headed for the kitchen, wondering what Charlotte had prepared for breakfast. He would have to leave soon.

He pinned his sheriff's badge to his waistcoat and sat down at the wooden table he'd made when he and Sarah had married.

Charlotte was no where to be seen. "Charlotte?" *Where on earth could she be?*

He went to the wood stove and picked up the kettle. Stone cold. The woman hadn't even lit the stove for his coffee. What was wrong with her? "Charlotte!" He needed to get her attention. Not that it would do him any good, he couldn't wait for coffee now. He'd have to get one at the diner in town.

He sighed. There was going to be a big learning curve with his new wife, he was certain.

He heard laughter, then Emma skipped into the room. "Mama and me have been playing games." She grinned broadly, and his heart skipped a beat. It was so good having his little girl living there. He'd missed her so much.

He squatted down to her level, and she put her little arms around his neck. "Where's Mama?" he asked softly.

"Fixing my cot," she whispered back. She kissed his cheek then ran off again.

He smiled, but his heart broke for the times he'd missed her growing up.

"Mama, Mama," Emma called. "Papa wants you." He watched as she skipped toward her precious Mama.

He stared as she walked toward him, a smile on her face. "You wanted me?"

"I have to go to work," he said with a heavy heart. He wanted nothing more than to stay home and get to know his new bride.

The closer she got to him, the more he wanted her. He lifted his hand and swept back a loose tendril that touched her cheek.

He wanted to touch that cheek right now.

He stepped toward her. They were so close he could feel her breath on his lips. He wanted so badly to kiss her lips.

She stared at him innocently.

He reached out and cupped her face in his hands. He leaned down and gently covered her lips. She tasted sweet, and her lips were soft.

He pulled back. He couldn't do this now. He had to go.

He looked into her caramel colored eyes, and his heart melted. He leaned in once more and claimed her lips.

She didn't resist.

"Eeeeeeeeeewwww! Papa, stop that!"

He felt a tug on his waistcoat. He looked down at the tiny interloper. "Get used to it sweetheart." He turned back to Charlotte, stole another quick kiss, then headed to the stables.

Angus had no idea why, but despite only knowing her a very short time, Charlotte seemed to tug at his heartstrings.

* * *

"Hellooooooooo."

Charlotte recognized Abigail's voice and headed toward the front door.

She greeted her sister-in-law with a warm hug. "Thank you again for yesterday. It was amazing," Charlotte told her.

Abigail shrugged as though it was nothing. From her experience, people only did things for you when they would get something out of it. But here it was different – they did things because they cared.

It was a huge change for Charlotte, and one she relished.

Abigail pushed her back. "My dear Charlotte, what on earth are you wearing?" She looked her up and down. "It looks like your Sunday best!"

Charlotte was in a pickle. "It's all I have," she said honestly. "I only managed to bring two outfits, apart from what I was wearing. I had to get away…" She stopped dead. She'd said too much.

Her sister-in-law's eyes opened wide. She jumped on Charlotte's words. "You had to get away? From what? Or perhaps from whom?"

Charlotte looked to the floor. "I didn't mean…"

She felt an arm go around her. "Your secret is safe with me, my dear. But we will have to properly outfit you. A trip to Dayton Falls is in order."

"Emma, come here, darling. We're going to town."

* * *

They stood at the counter of the Mercantile.

"Good morning, Mr Horvard," Abigail said. "This is Charlotte Doyle, my brother's new wife."

His expression was one of shock, but he was ever the professional. "Pleased to meet you, Missus Doyle," the owner said.

Abigail looked about the store. "We need some everyday dresses for Mrs Doyle, if you have some in stock."

Charlotte pulled on Abigail's sleeved arm. "I, I can't," she whispered. "What will Angus say?" She felt embarrassed that she even had to use his money to outfit her with clothes.

"You can, and you will." Abigail was adamant, and apparently Charlotte had no choice.

"Follow me," Mr Horvard told them. "I have a rack at the back of the store. If we don't have your size, I can order them in." He looked her up and down. "These should fit you though."

"Thank you, Mr Horvard. I'll let you know if we find anything."

Thoroughly dismissed, the store owner returned to the counter.

The two women scrounged through the racks. Abigail pulled a face, apparently not liking what she found. Emma held tightly to her Mama's hand.

Abigail finally pulled a dress from the rack. "This one," she said, holding it up in front of Charlotte. "This looks nice, and the color suits you."

Charlotte nodded but didn't commit.

"Oooh, here's another pretty dress for you."

By the time Abigail had finished, she had four pretty dresses she could wear at the cabin.

On their way back to the counter, they came across a box of lady's drawers on sale. Abigail picked up four pairs and handed those to Charlotte as well. "What? I'll bet you have virtually none with you."

Charlotte didn't deny it.

Mr Horvard wrapped the purchases and handed them over. "Put them on my brother's account."

 He nodded, then they left the store.

The three stepped outside, and Abigail pointed. "That's the Sheriff's Office over there," she said. "Want to visit Papa?" she asked Emma.

Of course, the child was excited to see her Papa. Strangely, Charlotte felt the same way.

The little girl ran through the door before anyone could stop her. "Papa! Papa!" She stood in the middle of the room. "Where's my Papa?" she asked when he was no where to be seen.

There was a clink of metal, then he walked in the room carry keys to the cells. "Did someone call Papa?" he asked, with a twinkle in his eye. He picked Emma up with one hand and held her tight. "I was putting a bad man in the cells," he explained.

Emma nodded, but Charlotte was sure she didn't understand.

He glanced across at her, and his eyes burned into hers. She tried to pull her gaze away, but it just wasn't happening.

He stepped toward her, his daughter still in his arms. "I've missed you today, darlin," he said quietly.

She wondered how that was possible after just one day. But oddly enough, she felt the same way.

His arm reached out and went around her, and he pulled her closer. "Now I have my two most favorite girls with me." He winked at his wife, who felt the heat creep up her face.

"All right, that's enough of the soppy stuff," Abigail said. "We came into town because Charlotte needed clothes." She pointed to the package. "And now we're going home. Goodbye, Angus." She turned tail and left the Sheriff's Office.

* * *

"You've never cooked before, have you?" Abigail asked.

Charlotte took great offense. "I have too. Cook taught me to bake cakes." She suddenly realized what she'd said, and her hands flew to her face.

Abigail frowned. "Cook? Only rich people have cooks…" Her hands went to her chest. "Oh my gosh, Charlotte. There's a lot you're not telling."

Charlotte closed her eyes tightly. She silently prayed for the Good Lord to give her the strength to get through this day. She didn't want to outright lie to Abigail, but she had to give her a plausible explanation.

"Please," she pleaded. "Don't tell Angus. I was in terrible danger if I stayed."

"You can tell me all about it while we collect vegetables from the garden." She picked up a basket and they headed outside.

"My dear girl, that is absolutely horrible. I am so glad you chose my brother to marry." She hugged Charlotte tightly, and it felt as though she would never let go. "You could have been his next victim."

"He was just after my inheritance, I'm certain," Charlotte told her. "He was thoroughly revolting, and evil. Thoroughly evil." She'd thought it before she found out about his two former wives and felt it even more after Miss Bethany had told her more.

"I'm so sorry you went through all that, Charlotte." She began to peel the potatoes. "I promise I won't tell my brother, but it's something you need to do."

"Once these are done we'll add the carrots and other vegetables." Abigail had placed the pot over the fire and added some water. "We always make more than we need, and then there's some left for breakfast."

Charlotte's heart sank. "I, I forgot to give him breakfast this morning." Tears filled her eyes.

Abigail patted her back. "He's resilient, he'll survive. But from now on, you make sure you have coffee and food ready for him each morning."

Charlotte nodded.

"The thing is," Abigail said, not meeting her eyes. "Our property is sold. William and I will be leaving soon, so I'm not going to be around to help you out. Or to teach you."

Charlotte gasped. *What was she going to do?* She was relying on Abigail to teach her how to be a good wife.

"I'll show you a few basics, but mostly you're on your own. I'm really sorry."

Charlotte threw the parsnips and turnips into the vegetable stew and stirred it as she'd been shown.

"This needs to cook for the rest of the day."

The other woman went to the pantry. Charlotte could see the dismay on her face. "There's virtually nothing here, and no bread." She pulled out flour and a few other ingredients and instructed Charlotte on how to make fresh bread.

"I'm never going to be able to do this," Charlotte wailed.

Abigail wiped her hands on her apron. "Of course you will. I'll write down the recipe for you, so you won't forget." She smiled at Charlotte, trying to reassure her, but Charlotte felt far from reassured right now.

Chapter Five

"This is delicious."

Charlotte leaned back in her chair and smiled. Her first meal as a married woman, and her husband liked it.

"Your sister helped," she said honestly. "I don't know what I'd do without her."

Emma sat watching the exchange between the two but didn't say a word. "Eat your stew, darlin," Angus told her.

"It's too hot, Papa."

He looked to Charlotte as though she would know what to do. She had no idea.

"Maybe blow on it?" It was the only thing she could think of. Emma smiled and did as she was told. Soon she was eating tiny bits of the stew.

"Oh my gosh!" Charlotte jumped up and pulled the bread out of the oven. "It's nearly burned. I totally forgot about it."

Angus looked back over his shoulder. "Nah, that's not burned. Just a bit… dark. It will be okay, I promise."

He got up from the table and got a wooden bread board and sharp knife, ready to cut the bread when it was cool enough.

Charlotte took the butter from the pantry, and placed it in front of her hungry husband, then took some plates from the cupboard.

There was an awkward silence. "This is one of my new dresses," she told him. "Do you like it?"

He looked her up and down. "It's pretty. Suits the color of your eyes."

"You're not mad?"

She stared at the floor.

"Why would I be mad? I want my beautiful wife to look her best." He held her hand and squeezed it. "Besides, what else do I get to spend my money on?" He leaned in and spoke quietly so only Charlotte could hear. "I don't suppose you bought some sexy nightwear?"

She was shocked, but he laughed.

She pulled her hand away in disgust.

"It was a joke, darlin," He was still laughing, and she was annoyed.

"I'm sure that bread is cool enough to cut now." She did her best to change the subject.

He gazed at his daughter. "Hurry up and eat, Emma. It's almost your bedtime." He glanced at her almost full plate. "That food must be cool by now."

He stood and cut the bread into thick slices. "Put some of this aside for the morning," he said. I'll have a few slices of bread and a hot cup of coffee before I leave."

He didn't say anything about not being fed this morning, but she knew exactly what he meant. "I'm sorry," she said. "It didn't enter my mind…"

He brushed her words aside. "You're new at this. You'll learn." He winked at her, and she was sure there was a double meaning in there somewhere.

He finished up his stew and bread, then stared at his wife. "I don't suppose that sister of mine made dessert?"

Charlotte was beaming, she knew she was, but she couldn't help it. "No, she didn't."

His smile disappeared.

"I did!" She was very pleased with herself too. "I made an apple pie using fruit from that big apple tree out the back."

Now he was beaming. "What a clever wife I have," he said, pulling her onto his lap.

Charlotte was beginning to feel that she did fit in.

* * *

"No! I don't want to!"

Charlotte wanted Emma to go outside with her, but the child stood her ground.

This was the first time she'd had any resistance or any sort of bad behavior from Emma. They'd become almost friends, and everything had been fine.

Until today.

She didn't know what to do, so she did the only thing she knew – she threated to punish the child. "This is your last chance, Emma," she said between ground teeth. "Either come outside with me now, or I'll take your toys away."

Emma glared at her. "No you won't," she yelled.

Charlotte stood glued to the spot. Becoming an instant Mama was never a good idea, and now she knew why.

Without another word, she stomped into Emma's room, and collected up all her toys. She put them on top of the wardrobe in the main bedroom and closed the door.

Now she was dealing with a tantrum. Emma lay on the floor of her room kicking and screaming and telling Charlotte what a horrible Mama she was.

It broke her heart, and hot tears streamed down her face, but she walked away.

She simply couldn't deal with the drama of it all. How was she going to be this child's Mama?

What would her mother have done? Charlotte thought back to all those years ago when *she* threw tantrums.

Her mother went about her business, and totally ignored her daughter. So that's what Charlotte decided to do.

She wiped at her face, picked up the basket and went outside, intent on collection the eggs from the hen house. The minute the front door slammed, the screaming stopped.

Charlotte continued to the hen house.

When she got there, she looked back toward the house, only to see two little eyes staring out at her.

Emma rubbed the tears from her eyes, and her Mama felt bad.

But only for a few moments. She realized this was not her fault, but the child's bad behavior that caused the problem.

She quickly turned away and went about her business – collecting up the eggs. Emma's most favorite thing to do.

Charlotte realized she'd become attached to the tiny girl in such a short time. Her heart was breaking that she was missing out on collecting the eggs from *secret hiding places*, as Emma called them, but she had a lesson to learn.

A tear trickled down her face. Being a parent was no easy task, as she was beginning to discover.

"Mama!" The little voice called to her from the porch. "I want to do that."

Charlotte swallowed. This was so hard. "Too late, Emma. You didn't want to come outside, so I did it myself." She had to stiffen her resolve and not let the child see how upset she was.

"But Mama…" Emma burst into tears. It was the hardest thing she'd ever had to do, not to cry in front of the small child.

Charlotte lifted her skirts against the filth of the hen house, and continued her task, then returned to the house.

Emma flung herself at her Mama the moment she returned. Putting the basket aside, Charlotte comforted the child. "Perhaps next time you'll do what you're told," she said, her voice breaking.

She was rewarded with a big hug, despite the sobs.

"Let's go and make a cake for Papa. We have lots of eggs."

Emma looked up at her with big blue eyes. Eyes that echoed her father's. "All right," she said with a wobbly voice, a stray tear trickling down her little face.

Charlotte sighed. She couldn't believe how much her life had changed from only a week ago.

* * *

"Chocolate cake," Angus said. "My favorite, especially when it's made by my two favorite girls."

Emma looked up at him and scowled. "Mama collected the eggs for the cake, she wouldn't let me."

She stomped her foot and pouted.

"But that's your favorite thing to do," he said, none too pleased. He glared at Charlotte.

She gasped.

She sat at the table and began to explain in a way Emma would also understand. "Emma was a very naughty girl today, and had a tantrum," she said. "She refused to go outside, and Mama had to collect the eggs instead."

His face softened. "You were being tested," he said quietly so Emma couldn't hear. "She's seeing how far she can push you." He grinned. "It sounds like you handled it beautifully."

He reached for a slice of chocolate cake. Charlotte slapped his hand. "Not now," she said playfully. "It's for supper."

He leaned in and whispered in her ear. "And what about after supper. Do you have something special for me then?"

They still hadn't consummated their marriage, and Charlotte knew it was wrong to keep him waiting. She was scared, even after what Abigail had told her.

She now knew it was natural, and how you got babies, but she still wasn't sure she wanted to do *that*. Even with her handsome husband.

She bit her lip, and felt his hand cover hers. "I promise not to hurt you, Charlotte," he said, and she nodded.

She dished up supper while Angus supervised Emma washing her hands. She knew she couldn't continue to avoid it.

Tomorrow was Sunday, and it didn't seem right to consummate their marriage on the Lord's day. She resolved to let him have his way with her that night.

* * *

Emma was tucked up and asleep in bed, and Charlotte could see the anticipation in Angus's eyes. There was no more avoiding it. They'd been married for nearly a week now and she'd not let him touch her in *that* way.

She began to undress for bed, but unlike other nights, he didn't leave the room.

"Let me help you with that," he said, unfastening her dress. She was nervous and could feel herself shaking.

Angus pulled her close and whispered to her. "It will be okay. Don't be nervous." He kissed her lips ever so lightly.

He pulled back, then slid her arms out of the sleeves and watched keenly as the garment fell to the floor.

"Such pretty under garments you have," he teased, pulling her chemise off.

He gently pushed her backwards onto the bed, having already pulled the covers back.

Angus lay beside her, his hands about her waist. He had promised to be gentle with her, and she had to believe he would.

* * *

Charlotte awoke in Angus's arms as she did most days, but today was different.

She was a woman now.

He'd promised to be gentle with her, and he was. The first time it had hurt, but after that it was wonderful. It made her wonder why she'd been so hesitant.

She gently pulled out of his arms, trying not to disturb him. But it wasn't to be. His arm snaked around her waist, and he pulled her back to his side.

Charlotte knew exactly what her husband wanted.

* * *

"We need to hurry," Angus said. "We're going to be late."

Charlotte pulled the bonnet on her head and straightened up Emma's dress. "I wonder whose fault that would be," she said, looking at him sideways.

It was, after all, Angus who pulled her back into bed.

Once outside, he lifted them up onto the wagon, pausing with Charlotte, to kiss her lips. She stared into his face. It was as though she was seeing him for the first time.

She knew it from the start, but he really was a handsome man. And strong. He could swing her up onto that wagon with absolutely no effort.

It was just a pity he didn't love her. That would be the icing on the cake.

Not that Mr Rainer had loved her. He was just an old pervert who wanted her parent's money and her inheritance.

Perhaps one day Angus would come to love her, and she him. Right now, she wasn't sure what she felt. She'd been thrust into being a bride so quickly, and everything had been like a blur.

It was only now she had time to think about her situation. Her life definitely wasn't as easy as it was before, with servants to undertake every task, even to the point of choosing her clothes each day.

Did she miss it? Most certainly.

Would she go back? Definitely not. She was happy here, even if her life was harder.

She did miss Allie though. She was always kind to Charlotte and protected her from her mother whenever she could.

"Did you hear what I said?" Angus's voice ripped through her thoughts.

She shook her head. "No, sorry. I was just thinking."

"We're almost there. Everyone at church is lovely, and I'm sure they'll welcome you with open arms."

Charlotte wasn't so sure. How did they feel about a complete stranger marrying one of their own?

Did anyone know she was a mail order bride? That probably disturbed her the most. She'd always looked down on mail order brides, but now she was one herself.

"Do they know?" she suddenly blurted out.

He glanced across at her. "That we're married? I should think so, by now."

She took a deep breath before asking the question. "That I'm a mail order bride." She felt the heat creep up her cheeks and put her hands to her face.

He reached across and pulled them down. "There's no need to be embarrassed. But no, they don't know." He squeezed her hand. "Frankly, it's none of their business."

"Whoa." He pulled the horses to a stop in a paddock next to the little church where they'd married. He climbed down, helped the others down, and pulled Charlotte close to him.

"I'm scared," she said quietly.

He grinned. "I recall you being scared about something else. And look how that turned out!"

Charlotte gasped. "You can't say things like that as we're walking into church. That's almost blasphemous."

He threw back his head and laughed. It was far from a laughing matter as far as Charlotte was concerned.

The organist began to play one of the hymns as they entered the chapel, and Angus guided her into a pew at the back.

Charlotte silently prayed to have a good life with Angus, and that he would eventually come to love her.

At the end of the service, Angus introduced her to the parishioners, but she knew their names would elude her for a while.

"Charlotte, come with Papa," he said, lifting his daughter, and giving his wife time to get to know some of the local women.

"You must join the ladies auxiliary, my dear," a much older lady, who introduced herself as Mrs Harrow, told her.

It would do her good to get out and meet other people, Angus had said. She was sure he was right.

Next time they would stay and have luncheon with the other members of the church. Today though, Angus said he just wanted to spend some time with his new family.

Mrs Mavis Jensen was the next to introduce herself to Charlotte. "I am Mrs Jensen," she said. "My husband is the undertaker."

Charlotte screwed up her nose.

"Yes, I know," Mrs Jensen said. "It is rather off-putting, but someone has to do it."

More of the women rallied around, and Charlotte was introduced. "Mrs Elizabeth Green, Mrs Annie Jackson, and Mrs Bertha Grogan," she said. "The doctor's wife."

Charlotte nodded but was almost certain she wasn't going to remember all their names.

Mrs Jackson stepped forward and leaned in close. "I think you're really brave taking on the Sheriff's daughter," she said. "You're only young yourself."

Charlotte bristled but knew Mrs Jackson was right. "She's a sweetheart," Charlotte said. "She's no trouble."

The women all nodded.

"Are you staying for luncheon today," Mrs Green suddenly asked.

"No, Angus wants to spend time together today. We'll stay next week though." The women all nodded and smiled, and Charlotte realized this could be her group of friends for many years to come.

"When does the ladies auxiliary meet?" she asked, genuinely interested.

"Wednesdays at 2," Mrs Harrow told her. "Can you cook, my dear?"

Charlotte blanched. "Of course," she said confidently. *Not really*, she said silently, but didn't want to show her naivety.

After chatting with her new friends for a good half hour, it was time for the ladies to set up for luncheon.

"My dear, why don't you convince Angus to stay?" Mrs Harrow made the suggestion and the others agreed.

Charlotte felt awful. "Why, we couldn't do that," she said meekly. "I haven't brought a contribution."

"Sheriff! Sheriff Doyle!" Mavis Jensen called him over. She continued when he was standing in front of her. "We've suggested you and your good wife stay for luncheon. I know you haven't brought a contribution today," she said quietly. "But there's plenty to go around. Mrs Doyle needs to get to know everyone, and they need to get to know her."

Emma clinging onto him, he stared across at Charlotte. "Is that what you want, darlin," he asked impassively.

She nodded, and he agreed.

It was mid-afternoon before they began to head home. Charlotte had enjoyed herself but was now tired. So was Emma, who rested her head on Charlotte's lap.

He reached across and squeezed her hand. "Did you enjoy yourself, darlin," he asked. "Some of those women can be a little overwhelming at times."

"Oh they can," Charlotte agreed. "But they are wonderful people. The sort who would do anything for you. At least they seemed at way." She felt wistful. "They're not like that back home."

He frowned at her. "They're not?" He was curious but she too tired to explain now. Besides Emma was sitting on her lap and she didn't want her to overhear.

"There are some horrid people where I come from," she said quietly. "Really selfish and self-serving."

"Want to talk about it?"

She stiffened. She really didn't. "Maybe another time."

He stared at her, then reached across and squeezed her hand. It was almost as though he understood.

* * *

Charlotte pulled the election cake out of the oven and sat it on the wooden board to cool.

"Hurry up and finish your food, Emma," she demanded. The child had been playing with her food for nearly half an hour. "We'll collect the eggs soon, then we'll be going to church."

Emma's eyes lit up. She loved playing with the other children at church. It must get lonely for her here at times, Charlotte thought. She knew she did at times.

She looked forward to church on Sunday when she got to spend time with her new friends. It was a bonus that Emma got to do the same thing.

Sitting around sharing food each woman had made was always a gift. You never knew what you would get, and it was a wonderful chance to try new foods. Sometimes she even managed to get the recipes.

She couldn't believe she'd been here a few months already.

She looked Angus up and down as he entered the kitchen. He scrubbed up really well – not that it was her first time noticing.

He wore the same outfit he'd worn on their wedding day, and she strongly approved. He came around behind her and put his arms around his wife.

"You are very special, Charlotte," he said, then kissed her gently on her shoulder.

She leaned back into him. "You are special too," she said quietly, meaning every word.

Emma's chair scraped along the floor as she shoved it back. "I'm finished," she said. "We can go to church now."

Charlotte stared at her. "Not in those clothes you won't! We'll collect the eggs and then you can change. *Then* we can go to church, and not a moment before."

Once they were ready, Angus lifted them up onto the wagon. Emma clung tight to her favorite doll.

At least they weren't late today, everyone was still entering the church. Angus parked the wagon and helped the others down, then they entered the church.

Charlotte listened to Onward Christian Soldiers playing in the background as they sat down, and pulled Emma closer. On the whole, she was well behaved in church, but every now and then she fidgeted. During those times, Angus reminded her the child wasn't quite three – she still had a lot to learn.

After the service was over, she stood in a huddle with her recent friends and chatted, as she did every Sunday before it was time for luncheon.

Emma had been running around beside them, playing with some of the other children. Suddenly she was gone.

Charlotte began to panic. "Angus! Emma is missing." Tears began to fill her eyes, and she could see the panic in his eyes, but Angus didn't show it.

"She'll be here somewhere. Probably playing with the other children."

They heard a scream. Charlotte gasped. "Emma!" She ran toward the sound, and found her daughter laying in the paddock, screaming in pain.

"I, I didn't see her there," Joe Hamish said. "I'm really sorry, Sheriff."

Angus waved off the man and hurried to his daughter. The doctor came rushing over and checked her for injuries.

"She's broken her leg," Doc Grogan said. "I'll splint it here. It will be too painful to move her."

Everyone stood in a huddle watching Emma's leg being splinted, and Charlotte felt ill.

She totally blamed herself. She took her eyes off the child for just moments, and now… She could have been killed. She held back a sob.

Angus must hate her. This was entirely her fault.

Mrs Jensen, one of the ladies from the auxiliary, came to comfort her. "She'll be fine. Old Doc Grogan will look after her. He's mended many a broken limb." She patted Charlotte gently on the back.

"It's my fault," Charlotte said quietly, tears threatening to break through.

The older woman must have seen her distress and lead her inside to sit down. "My dear Charlotte, children run off all the time. You can't blame yourself." Charlotte nodded but wasn't convinced.

Angus put his head around the entrance carrying Emma. "We have to go," he said briskly, and Charlotte knew it had already begun.

Her new husband hated her.

Chapter Six

Angus carried his daughter up the steps of the cabin, her little leg splinted for the break.

"Take it off, Papa, take it off." She had screamed the entire way home, and it was all Charlotte could do not to cry.

It was breaking her heart, and it was because of her. If she hadn't been busy talking with her friends, and had held tight to the child's hand, she'd be all right now.

She bit back a sob.

Angus carefully placed her on one of the soft chairs usually reserved for the adults. Wet eyes looked up at him, deploring him to remove the wretched thing from her leg.

Her little arms went up. "Please Papa, take it off." He squatted down to her level, and her arms went around his neck.

She could see the sadness in his eyes. "I'm sorry, Sweetheart. It has to stay – to fix your leg." And he really was sorry, she could see it etched on his face.

It made her feel even more guilty.

To think the poor baby was suffering because she didn't do the only thing she was tasked to do – care for his daughter.

She couldn't begin to imagine the pain she had suffered when that wagon wheel ran over her tiny leg. She ran from the room to prevent Angus from hearing the sobs she could no longer hold back.

She lay down on the bed and cried until she could cry no more.

She felt his presence before he approached her. "What's this then," he asked as he turned her to face him. "Emma will be fine. Doc Grogan said so."

But his eyes said what his words didn't. She was fully to blame.

She stared into his face as she lay there feeling helpless.

Helpless and guilty.

"She shouldn't have been hurt," she said quietly.

"No, but she was, so we have to deal with it." He didn't say as much, but he put the blame on her, as he should.

Tears welled up in her eyes once more. She'd tried to make this marriage work, but she'd let her husband down tremendously. And his daughter. His poor little girl would be maimed for life because of her stupidity.

She rolled away from him and let her tears flow. Before she knew it, she was sobbing uncontrollably.

Charlotte felt his hands go up around her, ever so gently. He turned her to face him. "Honestly, Charlotte, Emma is going to be alright. You heard the doc, a few weeks and the splint can come off."

But it didn't dissolve her feelings of guilt. "It's my fault!" The words were screamed, when she'd meant to say them quietly.

She felt him pull back quickly and turned to see his expression. It was shock.

For what felt like hours, but was really only minutes, he sat there staring at her. Then he shook his head, as if to clear his mind. Finally, he spoke. "How is it your fault," he asked quietly.

Another sob escaped her. "I'll leave, if that's what you want."

His eyes opened wide. "Why on earth would I want you to leave, Charlotte? *What did you do?*" She saw the pained expression on his face, and just wanted to run. As far away as she could get. But a part of her also wanted to stay.

She was falling in love with her husband and didn't want to leave him.

Her answer was so quiet she barely heard it herself. "I let go of her hand."

Before she knew what was happening, he scooped her up in his arms and held her tight. He didn't say a word, just sat there on the bed, and held her in his arms. "That's not your fault, Charlotte," he said quietly. "Children do such things."

"But I should have held her tightly." Tears streamed down her face.

He stared at her for long moments, then kissed her gently. "I'll hear none of this. Emma's injury is *not* your fault."

She swallowed hard. "So you don't hate me?" She stared at him, waiting to find out if she was to be banished.

"Hate you? Are you serious?" He glanced at her then looked away. "I could never hate you," he said quietly, then stormed out of the room, leaving Charlotte in his wake.

* * *

Angus left the room quickly. He couldn't stay in there another moment.

Seeing the torture on her face was agonizing. Blaming herself and putting herself through all that distress was almost the end of him. His heart was breaking.

He was a big strong man, but he nearly broke down in front of her, and that wouldn't do.

His darling Charlotte.

What did he do to deserve such a wonderful wife?

He loved Sarah, he really did, but he now knew it was not in the same way he loved Charlotte.

The moment he'd touched her at the railway station, when he'd lifted her onto the wagon, he felt the connection. They were meant to be. He wondered if she felt it too.

The way she stared into his face when he lifted her off the wagon, the way she pulled her hand back quickly when he touched her.

He always felt a ding when he touched her and wondered if she did too.

And the way she never resisted but instead leaned into him whenever he pulled her close.

There was a definite connection, he was certain of it.

It had been a massive change for both of them.

For him, it was bringing a stranger into his life, especially when getting a mail order bride was totally about bringing his daughter back home. But he had been willing to risk it.

For her, moving to a strange town, to an unknown home, and an equally unknown husband. All of which meant being far away from her family.

He appreciated all she'd been through these past months and wondered if they would endure for years to come.

He certainly hoped so. Even in this short time, he'd come to love Charlotte dearly.

* * *

It had been difficult for Charlotte, making the move to Dayton Falls. Effectively running away from home.

And to discover Angus had a daughter she was expected to raise? That was a huge shock.

But she'd managed.

Now she was suddenly plunged into desperation. Dear little Emma was in a splint and couldn't get around.

Desperate times called for desperate measures, and Charlotte couldn't leave the child inside for weeks on end. She already looked pasty and unwell.

She was delighted when Mrs Jensen, arrived a week later at the cabin bearing a carrot cake, *for our dear sheriff*, and a pram.

She'd frowned. What on earth was she going to do with a pram? Young Emma was almost three – she was beyond needing a pram.

"My dear girl," Mrs Jensen had said. "You can take little Emma for long walks." She leaned forward and touched the child's cheeks. "Look how pale and ill she looks. The child needs fresh air."

Charlotte stared at Emma's face. Mrs Jensen was right.

And so it began. Each morning after Angus left, Charlotte would make preparations for supper, do the laundry, then off they would go.

They would begin by strolling around the property, guessing the names of trees and other vegetation, and sometimes having a picnic at the nearby creek.

Angus had told her the creek was the culmination of the falls, which came down off the nearby Dayton mountains. That was where the town of Dayton Falls got its name.

It made perfect sense to her.

After their walk they would collect eggs from the hen house. Of course, the pram wouldn't fit in there, but Charlotte would pass the eggs out to Emma to look after. She loved seeing the delight on Emma's face – it was as though she'd collected them herself.

After their walk, which usually lasted at least an hour, they would return home and collect vegetables from the garden. These would be used for the next evening's supper.

"I think we'll make a rhubarb and apple pie for Papa's supper," Charlotte announced, collecting the necessary ingredients.

"Papa will be very happy," Emma announced. She loved nothing more than to make her Papa happy, and Charlotte felt exactly the same way.

* * *

Making love had become a regular occurrence, and as much as she thought she'd hate it, Charlotte came to enjoy it.

"We have to get out of bed," she told Angus. "I have to make your breakfast, and you need to get ready for work."

She left her husband alone and began to prepare an omelet. There were always plenty of eggs, and she was pleased Emma was still able to help her collect them.

She'd enjoyed her walks with Emma, and how close they'd become over the past weeks since her leg had been broken.

As she put more wood on the fire, she felt his strong arms go up around her waist. "I'm getting your coffee. Don't be impatient." She flicked his hands away.

"It's not coffee I want," he whispered.

She turned her head to see his grin.

"Papa, Mama!" Emma was awake.

"These mornings are getting colder," Charlotte said. "It seems to be much colder here in Dayton Falls than I remember in Westlake."

Angus placed Emma on the chair. "You're in Montana now, darlin'. It's always cold here in the winter."

"It will be Christmas soon," she said. "I guess it will get even colder?" Emma's eyes lit up.

"Christmas?" She could see the joy on the child's face.

Angus looked happy too. "Our first Christmas together," he said. "The three of us. Our little family."

Charlotte thought about Christmas with her family, and how stifled it always was. The amount of wasted food was criminal, and the only dispensation her father would allow was for the servants to have the left overs.

This year would be different. She knew it would.

"My only wish for Christmas, is that we spend it together," he said, despite it being some months away. "Just the three of us."

Charlotte handed him his coffee, his wish echoing her own.

Chapter Seven

Finally, the splint had come off, and things were back to normal.

Emma had relished running to the hen house to collect the eggs. Charlotte never let her go alone because of the risk of snakes and foxes. Angus had drummed that into her from the beginning.

It was almost time to leave for church, but Emma had insisted on collecting the eggs before they left. She'd persisted so much, and she could see Angus was getting agitated with the child's tomfoolery, so she finally gave in.

Emma was only steps ahead of her when she suddenly let out a high-pitched scream.

Charlotte was next to her in a flash. "What is it darling?" Emma was frozen but managed to point.

They both stood frozen to the spot.

Moments later, gunfire startled her. "Damned rattlesnakes," Angus said, as he used the barrel of the rifle to remove the offending creature.

"You said a naughty word, Papa," Emma said, visibly shaking from her frightening experience.

Angus leaned over and picked her up.

"Don't ever touch a snake, Emma," he said. "They'll kill you. But don't scream either, because they will rear up and attack."

Tears streaming down her little face, Emma nodded her head.

"Time to finish getting ready for church."

Charlotte pulled Emma's bonnet on and tied the bow, then tied her highly polished shoes. She pulled on her own bonnet, then they were ready to leave.

She looked her husband up and down. He really did scrub up well.

He watched her looking him over, and his eyes sparkled. Heat rose in her cheeks. "Like what you see, Charlotte?" He reached for her hand, then pulled her in to his side. She felt a familiar ding in her hand, then warmth spread through her body, as it always did when he touched her.

He spun her around until her back was against him. Without warning, he leaned down and kissed her neck. "I'm so glad you chose me," he said quietly.

His hands sat on her waist, holding her close. Then suddenly they were roaming her body. "Angus," she said sharply. "We have to go to church."

He pushed her gently away. "Let me look at you." He held her by the shoulders and held her slightly away from himself, so he could get a better look.

"You'll need new clothes soon," he said. "Go into the Mercantile tomorrow and get some new dresses. Bigger ones."

She frowned but nodded her agreement.

She had noticed she was putting on weight but had hoped Angus wouldn't.

She'd stood in front of the full-length mirror only yesterday and had frowned. She wasn't eating any more than she did at her parent's home, probably less, yet here she was, getting bigger by the week.

She'd guessed it was because she was happy. Ecstatic even.

"Angus," she said urgently. "We must leave *now*, or we'll be late." She picked up the apple pie she had made as their food share for luncheon after church.

It had become a regular occurrence for some months now, and Charlotte was enjoying getting to know the other parishioners of Dayton Falls.

* * *

"Thick vegetable soup and scones," Angus said as he tucked into his supper. "You really know how to reach a man's heart." He grinned at her then focused on her growing belly.

"I still don't understand why you didn't just tell me I was with child," Charlotte said, still annoyed at Angus for not saying anything.

"It was my little secret," he said, then tucked into his hearty soup again. "While I think of it, next Sunday after church we'll be working on the new room."

"New room? We?" *What was he talking about?*

"A group of the parishioners are coming out to help me build a new room for the baby."

Charlotte was taken aback. She'd never heard of such a thing before. "I thought the baby would be in our room, or in with Emma."

"Not in our room," he said quickly. "There are some things that have to stay private." He winked, and Charlotte felt the heat rise in her cheeks. She was very glad Emma had no idea what he was talking about.

"Christmas is just weeks away, and we want it finished before then." He reached for her hand. "The baby might be here by then. Doc Grogan says you haven't got long to go before he arrives."

"*He* might be a girl," she said teasingly.

Angus pulled her down into his lap. "No matter what it is, it will be *our* baby," he said. "And that's all that matters."

"We're having a little sister for me," Emma said, and apparently that ended the conversation.

Charlotte and Angus looked at each other and grinned.

* * *

Angus pulled Charlotte close to him as they lay in bed.

His arms wrapped around her, he wondered what he'd be doing right now if she hadn't agreed to be his mail order bride.

Or who he might have ended up with.

"We've been together for a long time now, Charlotte," he said quietly, as they lay there together. "You've never told me why you needed to get away in such a hurry."

She sighed, and he wondered if she would answer. "It's a long story, but my parents were going to marry me off to a revolting old man who'd already had one wife disappear and had the other one locked up in an asylum."

He tensed. No wonder she'd needed to leave with such haste.

"Plus, he was a disgusting pig."

If it hadn't been so serious, he might have laughed at her words.

"Charlotte," he said softly. "I'm glad you chose me." He baby kicked against his hands and it filled him with joy.

She wriggled backwards to get closer to him. "I'm glad I chose you, too," she said. "They had five potential husbands for me to choose from."

"And you chose me, out of all those men? Why?" He really was curious now.

She grabbed his hands that were wrapped around her swollen belly. "Because you sounded the nicest. And you were the sheriff – I knew you'd be strong and handsome."

He bit back his laughter – he didn't think she would appreciate it. "I'm glad," he said softly. "Charlotte," he said as he gently kissed her neck. "I know I haven't told you before, but I love you so much. My heart is filled with love for you."

He heard her gasp. "It didn't take long. You're such a wonderful woman, a perfect mother, and you're very special in many ways." He swallowed hard. Emotion threatened to overtake him.

"Hey, you're crying," he said, as he felt tears running down his arm. "Why are you crying? Isn't that a good thing?"

"I, I didn't know you felt that way," she said in a whisper. "I've loved you since almost the moment I met you. You were so caring from the start."

She rolled onto her back and looked into his eyes in the semi-darkness. "My life here is very different to when I lived with my parents, harder than before, but I wouldn't change it for anything."

He squeezed her hands. "Neither would I." He embraced her once more, and they fell into a deep sleep, wrapped in each other's arms.

* * *

Charlotte was amazed by the number of people who had arrived to help with the baby's room.

Mrs Jensen, whom she'd become close friends with, also came, along with a handful of the other ladies from the Dayton Falls church.

"You sit down and put your feet up, my dear," Mrs Jensen told her. "It's nearly your time. You need to take the load off your body."

She didn't argue – she knew they were right. She could feel she wasn't far off the birthing time and wanted to conserve her energy. Mrs Jensen had five children, so she knew best.

The older woman rummaged through her pantry until she found the ingredients she sought. "We women will have a baking afternoon, while the men do the hard work outside."

Charlotte nodded, feeling quite helpless.

"They'll be looking for something to eat when they're done," she said. Then she whispered loudly. "Men are always hungry." She wiped her hands on her apron and began mixing the ingredients for chocolate cake.

Mrs Green made bread, and Mrs Rowlands baked cookies. Charlotte had no idea that many people would fit in her little kitchen all at the same time.

Emma came running in to find out what everyone was doing. She looked very pretty in her floral short sleeved dress and matching bonnet. Her white pinafore was over the top of it.

"Mama," she said quietly as she tugged on Charlotte's hand. "Can I play outside?"

Charlotte opened her eyes. "Emma, you still have on your Sunday best," she said, horrified. "Sit down next to me for awhile. Mama is very tired."

"Mama," Emma said again, trying to climb up onto her Mama. "When is my little sister coming?" She kneeled on top of Charlotte now, her face very close to Charlotte's.

"Emma!" Mrs Jensen said sharply. "Get down off Mama this minute. You're going to hurt her."

Emma turned toward Mrs Jensen, and for a moment Charlotte was certain she was going to defy the older woman. She leaned in and kissed Charlotte gently on the cheek and climbed down.

It was all Charlotte could do not to cry.

Suddenly she screamed and held her belly. The three women ran toward her. They helped her to her feet and her waters broke.

"Get her into bed," Mrs Jensen said. "And someone get Angus. We need Doc Grogan."

Charlotte stifled a cry. She wasn't sure what was to come, but she was sure it wouldn't be pretty. No matter what, she was having Angus's baby, and that was all that mattered.

* * *

Angus sat on the porch praying.

He prayed Charlotte would survive the birth of this baby. He'd lost Sarah this way three years ago, and he didn't want to lose Charlotte.

His precious Charlotte.

He prayed for her to be strong enough to live through the ordeal, and for their baby to be healthy.

"Take Emma for a walk – far away from here," Mrs Jensen ordered him. "She doesn't need to hear this."

He grabbed the child's hand and began toward the creek. They were almost out of hearing when he heard an almighty scream.

He stood frozen to the spot and bowed his head. "Dear Lord," he whispered. "Please keep my Charlotte safe."

"Is Mama alright," Emma asked.

He looked down at the child. What was he to say? He leaned down and picked her up. "Mama is fine," he lied. "Our new baby is coming soon."

Emma's eyes opened wide. "Really? My baby sister is coming soon?"

She wriggled in his arms, wanting to get down. The moment she hit the ground her little legs took off running back toward the cabin.

"Emma," he called to her. "Stop now."

She defied him and kept running.

He had dealt with criminals who were more obedient than his little girl was right now, and it riled him up. At the same time, he understood her excitement. "Emma, stop," he said again. "Otherwise you will not be allowed to collect the eggs this week."

He hoped it would be enough. It was her most favorite thing to do.

He shaded his eyes from the sun trying to see her. As he got closer, he could see the child had stopped. Thank goodness Charlotte had told him her secret weapon to getting Emma to behave.

He grinned momentarily, then his face stiffened, remembering the situation Charlotte was in right now.

"Come back," he called, waving to her. "We'll go to the creek for a while."

Face dropping, the child returned to her father. "Do you know the way," he asked. "I'm not sure I do."

Of course, he knew, but needed to keep her occupied.

She was excited to show him how to reach the creek she enjoyed so much.

He sat on a log near the water, watching Emma play. As the sun got lower behind the Dayton Falls Mountains, he decided it was time to go back.

At least he hoped it was.

He wasn't sure what he would find but hoped with all his heart his darling Charlotte was still of this world. He couldn't bear to lose her. His only saving grace was he'd found the strength to tell her how much he loved her.

As they approached the house, Mrs Jensen stood on the porch. His heart beat quickened.

She wasn't smiling, she was just standing there.

His head was spinning, and he felt a little faint. He tightened his grip on Emma's tiny hand.

He was only steps away from the cabin when Mrs Jensen sprung toward him.

"Congratulations, sheriff," she said, beaming. "You have a beautiful baby boy."

His heart beat quickened again. *What about his wife? What wasn't she telling him?*

He tried to push his way up the steps, but Mrs Jensen was having none of it. "Charlotte needs to rest," she said quietly.

"She survived?" he asked quietly. "My beautiful wife is alive?"

Tears threatened to push through, but he wasn't letting Mrs Jensen see his weakness. He turned toward Emma. "We'll go and collect the eggs now," he told her softly.

Mrs Jensen smiled knowingly, and he pulled Emma behind him. "We don't have the egg basket," Emma said, pouting at him.

"We'll use your pinafore to carry them," he told her.

His Charlotte was alive. He couldn't ask for anything more.

* * *

"Joseph Doyle. I like it," Angus said.

He pulled back the blanket slightly and gazed down at his new son. He was amazing. Just like his mother.

"I wanted a sister," Emma said, pouting. Then she stomped her foot.

"We don't get choices, Emma," Angus told her, touching her nose with his finger. "Maybe next time it will be a little sister." Charlotte glared at him.

Joseph began to wail. "He's probably hungry," Charlotte told him.

He sent Emma to her room to play while Charlotte fed their baby. Angus sat on the side of the bed watching her breast feed him. Their little miracle.

He was so grateful for his wonderful wife and their beautiful family.

Christmas was two days away, and his wish was about to come true. Only instead of being the three of them, they were now four.

His heart was overwhelmed with joy.

Epilogue

Two years later…

"Papa, it's snowing!" Five-year-old Emma shouted.

Two-year-old Joseph ran shakily across the room, trying to reach his Mama who was holding twelve-month-old Grace.

Charlotte sat with her feet up, her eyes opening and closing as she drifted in and out of sleep.

"Another Christmas almost here, and another baby about to arrive," Angus said lovingly.

They'd had to add another room to accommodate their every-growing brood.

"This is the last baby, Angus," Charlotte said sharply.

Angus laughed. "That's what you said last year and look at you now." He grinned at her, knowing she would forgive him in a heart beat.

She sat watching out the window, mesmerized by the snow.

Charlotte loved her little family. She loved and adored her husband and knew the best thing she'd ever done in her life was become a mail order bride.

If she hadn't, she would never have met her amazing husband, nor would she have all these beautiful children.

The Lord's gifts were truly bountiful.

From the Author

Thank you so much for reading my book – I hope you enjoyed it.

I would greatly appreciate you leaving a review where you purchased, even if it is only a one-liner. It helps to have my books more visible!

~*~

The next book in this series is The Barber's Christmas Bride

About the Author

Multi-published, award-winning and bestselling author Cheryl Wright, former secretary, debt collector, account manager, writing coach, and shopping tour hostess, loves reading.

She writes both historical and contemporary western romance, as well as romantic suspense.

She lives in Melbourne, Australia, and is married with two adult children and has six grandchildren. When she's not writing, she can be found in her craft room making greeting cards.

Links

Website: *http://www.cheryl-wright.com/*

Facebook Reader Group:
https://www.facebook.com/groups/cherylwrightaut hor/

Join My Newsletter:

https://cheryl-wright.com/newsletter/
(and receive a free book)

www.ingramcontent.com/pod-product-compliance
Lightning Source LLC
Chambersburg PA
CBHW071537100726
47908CB00004B/1416